CURIOUS SCIENTISTS

AMAZING LIFE SCIENCE ACTIVITIES

Rani Iyer

raintree

a Capstone company — publishers for children

Raintree is an imprint of Capstone Global Library Limited, a company incorporated in England and Wales having its registered office at 264 Banbury Road, Oxford, OX2 7DY – Registered company number: 6695582

www.raintree.co.uk
myorders@raintree.co.uk

Edited by Anna Butzer
Designed by Heidi Thompson
Picture research by Morgan Walters
Production by Kathy McColley
Originated by Capstone Global Library Limited
Printed and bound in China

ISBN 978 1 4747 4266 5
21 20 19 18 17
10 9 8 7 6 5 4 3 2 1

Coventry City Council	
CEN*	
3 8002 02357 068 4	
Askews & Holts	Jan-2018
J570.78 JUNIOR NON-F	£11.99

British Library Cataloguing in Publication Data
A full catalogue record for this book is available from the British Library.

Acknowledgements
We would like to thank the following for permission to reproduce photographs: Capstone Studio, Karon Dubke. Shutterstock: amgun, (gears) design element throughout

All the Internet addresses (URLs) given in this book were valid at the time of going to press. However, due to the dynamic nature of the Internet, some addresses may have changed, or sites may have changed or ceased to exist since publication. While the author and publisher regret any inconvenience this may cause readers, no responsibility for any such changes can be accepted by either the author or the publisher.

CONTENTS

Curious life 4

Watch seeds sprout 6

Staying warm in the Arctic. 8

A frog's trick to surviving winter 10

Eat like a bird 12

Cactus survival 16

The changing colours of leaves. 18

Mouldy bread 20

Glossary. 22

Find out more. 23

Index 24

CURIOUS LIFE

Do you wonder about the plants and animals living in the world around you? Do you ask questions about life cycles? Can something be both living and non-living? To find out the answers to questions like these, curious scientists do experiments.

Now it's your turn to be a curious scientist. Get ready to use your creativity and get a little messy! You will find out what it's like to eat like a bird and discover how frogs stay warm in cold weather. The results of your experiments will be amazing!

Safe science

Read through each activity before starting. Collect all of the materials that you will need. You may need an adult to help you find or buy some materials. Experiments can be tricky. Be sure to ask an adult for help if you need it.

WATCH SEEDS SPROUT

Ever wonder what happens after you plant a seed in the ground? This experiment will show you what is going on underground! Watch seeds **germinate** before your eyes. Then see your plants grow each day.

Materials:

- water
- 1-2 paper towels
- jar
- 2-3 seeds (sunflower, popcorn, peas or beans)

Steps:

1. Dampen two to three paper towels. Ring out the paper towels so no excess water sits in the jar. Place the paper towels in the jar.
2. Place the seeds in the jar. Position them in different places inside the jar towards the outside so you can see them.
3. Place the jar near a window that gets plenty of sunlight.
4. Check back after a couple of days. What do you see?

Step 2

How it works:

All seeds need moisture, clean air and the right temperature to germinate. With the right conditions the plant inside starts to grow and get bigger. Moisture comes from the wet paper towels. The right temperature is created when the jar is placed near a window that gets sunlight. Clean air is also inside the jar. All the things needed for the seeds to germinate are inside the jar. It breaks out of the seed coat. Roots reach down and a **shoot** grows up. After about five to six days, take your growing plants out and place them in soil. Growing plants need the nutrients from soil and sunlight to survive.

germinate when a seed sends out a root and a stem
shoot the white stem growing out of a seed that becomes a plant

STAYING WARM IN THE ARCTIC

The Arctic is a **frigid** place on Earth. Many animals live on land and in the freezing water. Polar bears, whales, harp seals and walruses are some animals that live in the Arctic. In this activity, you will discover how these animals stay warm in cold **climates**.

Materials:

- four plastic zip-top bags
- 280 grams (1½ cups) lard
- spoon
- large bowl
- ice cubes
- water
- stopwatch
- paper and pencil

Steps:

1. Turn one of the zip-top bags inside out and place it in another bag. Line the zip-tops up so you can zip the bags together.
2. Using the spoon, put the lard in between the two bags. Spread the lard around to create a layer between the two bags. Zip the bags together.
3. Do the same thing with the other two zip-top bags, but don't add the lard.
4. Fill a large bowl with ice cubes and water. It should be deep enough for your hands to be fully underwater.
5. Put your hand in the plain zip-top bag and put it in the ice water. Use the stopwatch to time how long you can keep your hand in before it gets too cold.

Step 1

6. Remove your hands when you get uncomfortable. Stop your stopwatch and write down the time.

7. Now put the same hand in the zip-top bag with the layer of lard. Put it in the ice water. Use the stopwatch again to time how long you can keep it in the water. Record your results.

8. Look at your data. Were you able to keep your hand in the ice water longer using the zip-top bag with the layer of lard? What was the time difference?

How it works:

Animals living in cold places develop several **adaptations** to live in their climate. One adaptation is to develop a layer of fat under the skin called blubber. The fat keeps the animal's body insulated in cold climates. Lard is a type of fat. When you added lard to the zip-top bags, you protected your hand from the cold. Therefore, you were able to keep your hand in cold water for a longer time.

frigid very cold in temperature

climate the usual weather that occurs in a place

adaptation a change a living thing goes through to better fit in with its environment

A FROG'S TRICK TO SURVIVING WINTER

In winter, you might bundle up with a winter jacket, a hat and gloves. But some frogs use what they have inside their bodies to stay warm. In this experiment, you will discover the chemicals that frogs use to keep from freezing.

Materials:

- two small, clear freezer-safe containers with lids
- 240 millilitres (1 cup) water
- kitchen scale
- paper and pencil
- 240 millilitres (1 cup) maple syrup
- freezer
- bowl

Steps:

1. Pour the water into one of the containers. Place the container on the scale. How much does it weigh? Write it down. Put the lid on tight.
2. Pour the maple syrup into the other container. Place on the kitchen scale. Write down the weight. Snap the lid on tightly.
3. Put the two containers in the freezer.
4. Wait five to six hours.
5. Remove the containers carefully from the freezer.
6. Place the water container on the kitchen scale. Has the weight changed? Do the same with the syrup.

Step 2

7. Which is heavier? Was the container with water heavier after you froze it?
8. Open the container with water. Are you able to pour it into the bowl? Is the water frozen? Set the container aside.
9. Open the container with syrup. Does the syrup pour into the bowl?
10. What does the syrup contain that the water does not have? Taste the syrup and water to find out the difference.

How it works:

Animal cells have water. If the cells freeze, the animal can die. Freezing increases weight and causes water to expand. During winter some frogs produce a lot of a type of sugar called **glucose**. It keeps their blood from freezing. Even when the outside of the frog's body freezes, the cells remain alive due to glucose. In this experiment, it was the sugar in the maple syrup that kept it from freezing.

glucose a natural sugar that gives energy to living things

EAT LIKE A BIRD

Every bird has a certain way of eating. A hummingbird has a beak that is long and thin. This helps it dip into flowers to sip nectar. An eagle swoops on its **prey** in the air or dives to the ground to pick it up. In this activity, you will learn how birds' adaptations help them survive.

Materials:

Food

- marshmallows
- salad leaves
- rice
- peanuts in shells or pistachios in shells
- fruit juice
- paper and pencil

Bird beaks

- tweezers
- chopsticks
- tongs
- pliers
- straw

Steps:

1. Arrange the food in an orderly manner.
2. Write down the order in which they are all arranged.
3. Use each of the 'beak' items to pick up the food.
4. Write down or describe what happens when you pick up the food with one of the 'beak' items.

Examples of what you might observe:

- It is hard to use chopsticks to break open the shells of nuts.
- The tongs are too big to pick up pieces of rice.
- It is easy to crack open the nuts with the pliers.

Now list the other things you observed.

How it works:

Different birds have different beaks. They come in many shapes and sizes. All birds have specialized beaks that help them find food and eat in the place they live. The place they live is called a **habitat**. Woodpeckers have a tweezer-like beak. They can peck holes in dead trees and grab the tiny insects living inside. The pliers are like the powerful beak of a cardinal. They crack open pistachio nuts.

habitat the natural place and conditions in which a plant or animal lives

CACTUS SURVIVAL

Have you ever forgotten to water a plant and it started to die? Plants need water to survive! But cactuses are known for living in desert climates. In this activity, you'll discover how a cactus can live in such a hot and dry place.

Materials:

- felt-tip pen
- scissors
- two sponges
- paper and pencil
- measuring cup
- water
- two plastic cups
- kitchen scale
- baking tray
- wax paper

Steps:

1. Draw the shape of a cactus on one of the sponges. Cut it out.
2. Place it on top of the second sponge and trace around it. Cut out the second sponge cactus. This way the sponges will be about the same size. Weigh each sponge and record the weight.
3. Put 80 millilitres (1/3 cup) of water in each plastic cup. Place a sponge cactus into each cup and set aside for one hour.

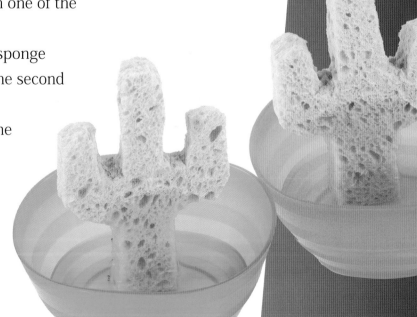

4. Remove each sponge and weigh it. Write down your observations.

5. Set the cactus sponges onto the baking tray. Wrap one of the sponges with a sheet of wax paper.

6. Check on your cactus sponges for a few days. Weigh the sponges each day. Which sponge dried out faster?

How it works:

Cactuses go through a process called **photosynthesis** just like other plants. They need the sun for energy. They also need water to survive. But how do cactuses that live in the desert survive during long periods of time without any water? They have adapted to their environment. Cactuses store water inside and save it for later. The waxy coating of a cactus helps keep the water from **evaporating**. Similarly, the waxed paper helped the sponge hold moisture.

photosynthesis process by which plants make food using sunlight, carbon dioxide and water

evaporate process of change in water from a liquid to a gas

THE CHANGING COLOURS OF LEAVES

You know that summer is over and autumn is starting when the leaves on trees begin to change. Green leaves turn orange, red, yellow and brown. This easy **chromatography** activity will show you how to find the hidden colours in leaves.

Materials:

- several leaves from two to three different trees, found on the ground
- two to three small glasses or jars with lids
- spoon
- surgical spirit
- dish
- hot water
- scissors
- white paper coffee filters
- tape
- pencil

Steps:

1. Tear the leaves into pieces and place them in the jars. Use the back of the spoon to crush the leaves up even more.
2. Pour just enough surgical spirit into the jars to cover the leaves.
3. Cover the jars with their lids or cling film.
4. Put the jars in a dish of hot tap water. Let them sit for about 30 minutes or until the surgical spirit turns green.

Tip: Keep leaves from different trees separate as you collect them.

5. Cut a few strips of filter paper about 5 centimetres (2 inches) wide. Tape the strips to a pencil.
6. Uncover the jars and set the pencil across. Let the strip just barely touch the liquid.
7. Let the filter strips sit in the mixture for at least two hours.
8. Take them out and let them dry.

How it works:

Plants use photosynthesis to convert the sun's rays into food. To absorb the light, leaves use their brightly coloured **pigments**. Even though a leaf looks like it is mostly one colour, it actually has different pigments that you can't see. The most important pigment is **chlorophyll**. In the autumn, the chlorophyll begins to break down. That is when we start to see the leaves changing colour. What are the different bands of colours on the filter strips? These are the different pigments in the leaves. This experiment will help you predict what colour the leaves will be in the autumn.

chromatography a process for separating different components from a mixture

pigment a substance that gives something a particular colour when it is present in it or is added to it

chlorophyll the green substance in plants that uses light to make food from carbon dioxide and water

MOULDY BREAD

It's lunchtime. You sit down and are about to start eating. Wait! Did you wash your hands? Your skin is home to billions of **bacteria**. But when your hands don't look dirty it is easy to forget about the bacteria you can't see. This activity will show you how quickly bacteria grows.

Materials:
- three zip-top sandwich bags
- permanent marker
- tongs or disposable gloves
- three slices of bread
- water in a spray bottle
- soap and water for hand washing
- paper towel

Steps:
1. Use the permanent marker to label the zip-top bags. Label them 'not touched', 'dirty hands' and 'clean hands'.
2. Use the tongs or gloves to take one slice of bread and put it inside the zip-top bag labelled 'not touched'. Make sure you don't touch the bread or the inside of the bag with your fingers!
3. Spray the bread with two sprays of water and seal the bag.
4. Take the next slice of bread and touch it with your bare hands. Put the bread inside the bag labelled 'dirty hands'. Spray the bread with two sprays of water and seal the bag.

5. Wash your hands with soap and water and dry them with a paper towel. Take the last slice of bread and put it in the bag labelled 'clean hands'. Spray the bread twice and seal the bag.

6. Check the bags for the next six to seven days. What do you see?

How it works:

Mould will grow on all three slices, but more mould will appear sooner on the slice that you touched before you washed your hands. Mould is a tiny, living **organism** that gets its energy from the material on which it grows. Mould is able to grow on objects that have small amounts of living material. The mould grew quicker on the slice that was touched with dirty hands because of the bacteria on it.

Not touched

Clean hands

Dirty hands

bacteria one-celled, tiny living things; some are helpful and some cause disease

organism a living thing such as a plant, animal, bacterium or fungus

21

GLOSSARY

adaptation change a living thing goes through to better fit in with its environment

bacteria one celled, tiny living things; some are helpful and some cause disease

chromatography process for separating different components from a mixture

chlorophyll the green substance in plants that uses light to make food from carbon dioxide and water

climate the usual weather that occurs in a place

evaporate process of change in water from a liquid to a gas

frigid very cold in temperature

glucose a natural sugar that gives energy to living things

germinate when a seed sends out a root and a stem

habitat the natural place and conditions in which a plant or animal lives

organism living thing such as a plant, animal, bacterium or fungus

photosynthesis process by which plants make food using sunlight, carbon dioxide and water

pigment substance that gives something a particular colour when it is present in it or is added to it

prey an animal hunted by another animal for food

shoot the white stem growing out of a seed that becomes a plant

FIND OUT MORE

READ MORE

101 Great Science Experiments (DK Children, 2015)

Experiments with Plants (Read and Experiment), Isabel Thomas (Raintree, 2016)

Outdoor Science Lab for Kids, Liz Lee Heinecke (Quarry Books, 2016)

WEBSITES

www.bbc.co.uk/bitesize/ks2/science/living_things
Play games about living things, read the science behind them and then take a quiz to check what you've learned.

www.scienceprojectideas.co.uk/biology-category.html
Grow yeast, make a rubber band from dandelions and test the strength of paper in these biology experiments.

www.science-sparks.com/category/key-stage-2
Carry out fun experiments, such as investigating earthquakes using sweets and testing car safety using toys, on this website.

INDEX

adaptations 9, 12, 17
animals 8, 9, 10, 11, 12, 15

bacteria 20, 21
blubber 9

cactuses 16, 17
cells 11
chemicals 10
chlorophyll 19
chromatography 18
climates 8, 9, 16

glucose 11

habitats 15

organism 21

photosynthesis 17, 19
plants 6, 7, 19

safety 5